For Lina

KINGFISHER
Larousse Kingfisher Chambers Inc.
95 Madison Avenue
New York, New York 10016

First American edition 1994
2 4 6 8 10 9 7 5 3 1

Text and illustrations © Peter Cottrill 1994

Library of Congress Cataloging-in-Publication Data
Cottrill, Peter.
Anteater on the stairs / by Peter Cottrill. — 1st American ed.
p.   cm.
Summary: Joe, a new neighbor, tells Sophie stories about his
fabulous pets but is unprepared when he meets her own pet Snowy.
[1. Pets—Fiction.   2. Honesty—Fiction.]   I. Title.
PZ7.C82985An   1994
[E]—dc20   93-41505   CIP   AC

ISBN 1-85697-976-8

Printed and bound in Italy

Anteater on the Stairs

Peter Cottrill

Kingfisher

NEW YORK

Sophie was just moving into her new home when
Joe turned up and decided to introduce himself.
"I'm Joe from number 47," he said.

"They all know me around here. My father's a world-famous naturalist and we've got some of the weirdest and rarest animals you've ever heard of."

"What kind of animals?" asked Sophie.

"Tropical fish,
poisonous snakes,
flying squirrels,
a giant tortoise,
an arctic wolf,
fruit bats,
tree frogs,
piranhas,
iguanas,
chameleons,
an octopus,
and a
big baboon."

"Amazing!" said Sophie. "I—"
"And that's not all," said Joe.

"There's Beaky, my giant Venezuelan anteater.
He's always sniffing around the stairs...

...and Snapper, my Egyptian crocodile.
He loves breakfast in the bathtub...

...and Prince, my Bengal tiger. He likes the wildlife programs on TV...

...and Zanzibar, my African elephant. He helps
me clean Mom and Dad's car...

...but my favorite of all is Tarquin, the sperm whale. Dad's had a giant pool built especially for him on our roof."

"Incredible," said Sophie.

"I know," replied Joe. "I don't suppose you have any pets."

"Just Snowy," said Sophie. "He's—"

"Tell you what," interrupted Joe, "I'll bring Prince and
Zanzibar over to see you first thing in the morning.
That'll be a treat for you."

"Great," said Sophie. "I'm sure Snowy will be pleased, too."

The next morning Sophie waited and waited
and waited for Joe. When he didn't turn up
she decided to visit his house instead.

"I'll buy Snowy's breakfast at the same time,"
she thought, and wrote a list. She shouted
goodbye to Snowy and set out.

Joe's house seemed very quiet and ordinary. There were
no signs of roaming tigers or sounds of trumpeting elephants.
Joe's mom answered the door. "I think he's
upstairs, dear. Why don't you go see?"

Sophie climbed the stairs
half expecting to meet an
anteater. But she didn't.

She looked in the
bathroom. But there was
no Egyptian crocodile.

She looked on the roof.
But there was no whale.

Then she found Joe's
room.

There was no Joe but
there were plenty of
animals.

An anteater,
a crocodile,
a tiger,
an elephant,
a whale,
tropical fish,
poisonous snakes,
flying squirrels,
a giant tortoise,
an arctic wolf,
fruit bats,
tree frogs,
piranhas,
iguanas,
chameleons,
an octopus,
and a big baboon.

But not one of
them was real.

Sophie left Joe's house. So that's it, she thought.
On her way home she stopped off to buy Snowy the
largest juiciest fish she could find.

Joe was waiting for her when she got back.

"Hi, Sophie! Guess you're wondering why I couldn't make it this morning. Prince and Zanzibar were in such a boisterous mood that I thought it might be a little dangerous for you."

"Really?" said Sophie. "Never mind, you can help me feed Snowy now you're here."

"No thanks," said Joe. "I've got Snapper to feed and Prince to brush and—"

"Come on," interrupted Sophie. "It won't take very long."

"Isn't that fish just a little bit big for Snowy?"
chuckled Joe.

"Oh, no," said Sophie. "This is just a snack."